THE CLONE WARS™

INTERGALACTIC ADVENTURE
ACTIVITY BOOK

Grosset & Dunlap · LucasBooks

This book is published in partnership with LucasBooks, a division of Lucasfilm Ltd.

Copyright © 2008 Lucasfilm Ltd. & ® or ™ where indicated. All Rights Reserved. Used Under Authorization. Published by Grosset & Dunlap, a division of Penguin Young Readers Group, 345 Hudson Street, New York, New York 10014. GROSSET & DUNLAP is a trademark of Penguin Group (USA) Inc. Printed in the U.S.A.

The publisher does not have any control over and does not assume any responsibility for author or third-party websites or their content.

ISBN: 978-0-448-44997-5   10 9 8 7 6 5 4 3 2

CODE BREAKER

Use the code below to find the name of the dark assassin and Anakin Skywalker's archenemy!

A	B	C	D	E	F	G	H	I	J	K	L	M
1	2	3	4	5	6	7	8	9	10	11	12	13

N	O	P	Q	R	S	T	U	V	W	X	Y	Z
14	15	16	17	18	19	20	21	22	23	24	25	26

1   19   1   10   10   22   5   14   20   18   5   19   19

___ ___ ___ ___ ___   ___ ___ ___ ___ ___ ___ ___ ___

2

MISSION CRITICAL

You're out on an important mission and it's time to report back to base. Study this page carefully and then turn the page over to answer the questions asked by Jedi Master Obi-Wan Kenobi.

MISSION DEBRIEFING

You hear a sharp crackle through your communications device and suddenly you're being urgently questioned by Obi-Wan. Answer the questions below—remember, no peeking at the previous page!

1. How many ships can you see in your midst? _____

2. What color is the planet on your top right? _____

3. Can you see a sun nearby? _____

4. We have reports of asteroids in the vicinity. How many can you see from your current location? _____

5. Watch out for enemy ships close by. What colors are the lights of the ship closest to you? _____

6. Is there something wrong with your laser cannons? What color is the the light below your control levers? _____

PERILOUS ESCAPE!

Anakin and Ahsoka are lost in an asteroid belt! Plot their escape with your finger, but remember: Only one path leads to safety . . .

CRAZY CLONING

The Galactic Senate authorized the cloning of one of their greatest military leaders, General Grievous, but something went wrong. Can you find the five differences between the real General Grievous and the fake?

THE CONSTELLATION

Use a pen to connect the stars and reveal planet Dagobah's biggest hero!

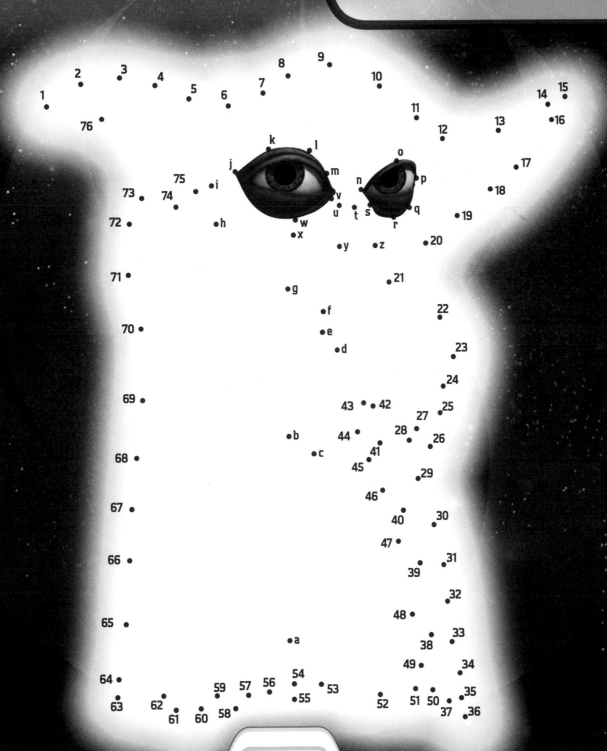

CALLING ALL OCCUPANTS!

Make your own cool wrist-radio communicator. When you're fighting battle droids with a lightsaber in one hand and a blaster in the other, it helps to have a hands-free device when calling for backup!

You'll need: safe scissors, tinfoil, string, buttons, small plastic bottle lids, and glue or sticky tape.

1. Cut out the wrist-radio communicator on the next page and fold it around your arm one and a half times.

2. Now, make a small cut $3/4$ inch from both ends—see the diagram opposite and be extra careful not to cut all the way through!

3. You can decorate your wrist-radio with tinfoil and plastic lids for buttons. Use plain string or string wrapped up in tinfoil to create wiring.

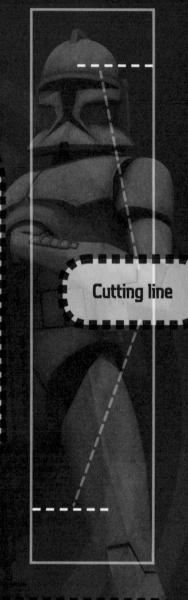

Cutting line

4. Fasten the communicator by slipping the two cut edges together. Now you're ready to broadcast!

Ask an adult to help you with this activity.

TK-421

COPY THAT, OVER!

Captain Rex finds himself outnumbered by battle droids! Use a pen to clone him by copying each square into the blank grid. But be quick—time is running out!

ON THE DARK SIDE

Test your trained Jedi-eye by looking carefully at these shadows. Then write the names of the characters on the lines underneath.

1. _____

2. _____

3. _____

4. _____

5. _____

Jedi Master Mace Windu has an urgent transmission that must get through to Anakin! Beginning at START, cross out every third letter to help R2-D2 decode the message.

START M A T Y T F H E K F O M R C S E B N E W L L I P H Y T O U

___ ___ ___ ___

___ ___ ___

___ ___ ___ ___

___ ___ ___ .

UPSIDE DOWN IN SPACE

Find the words in this galactic search!

S	L	I	G	H	T	S	A	B	E	R	A
U	P	P	H	Z	M	J	E	D	I	N	I
O	U	R	E	J	F	A	P	X	A	G	N
V	Z	H	S	W	R	A	L	K	A	Z	D
E	X	Q	U	S	L	E	I	C	H	L	N
I	R	U	U	T	E	N	X	A	S	P	O
R	S	N	Y	K	T	R	Q	X	O	Y	B
G	T	E	M	Y	A	L	T	Q	K	X	I
N	M	Y	N	T	I	B	E	N	A	Q	W
A	W	R	J	O	H	K	B	T	E	R	A
P	C	J	H	J	L	W	Y	A	T	V	N
L	I	V	H	X	U	C	G	M	J	E	B

AHSOKA
ANAKIN
CLONES
GRIEVOUS
HUTTLET
JABBA

JEDI
LIGHTSABER
OBI-WAN
REX
VENTRESS

COLOR THEIR WORLDS!

There are millions of planets, moons, suns, and star systems revolving in space. Color in the planets as you think they would look, using the descriptions as a guide.

Tatooine
Obi-Wan hid the infant Luke Skywalker on this remote desert planet with two suns. Home of nomadic Tusken Raiders, Jawa clans, and shadowy characters.

Alderaan
Princess Leia grew up on this peaceful planet with no moons. It is covered by grasslands, jungles, small seas, and majestic mountains.

Moon of Endor
Covered in lush forests, with polar caps at the north and south poles, this planet is home to the fiendishly clever Ewoks.

Hoth

The Rebel Alliance had their secret base hidden on this frozen world of ice caves and snowy peaks.

Dagobah

A planet of swamps and mists and home to a variety of slugs, gnarled trees, prehistoric vines, and a small, wise Jedi Master named Yoda.

The Death Star

Not strictly a planet, more a giant weapon with enough firepower to destroy an entire planet! Invulnerable to a large-scale attack, Luke Skywalker and a small band of Rebels, flying single-seat X-wing and Y-wing starfighters, set out to blow it up.

SIGNAL SCRAMBLE

Use the clues to unscramble the names!

Anakin Skywalker's
right-hand student:

ASHAKO

_____

Astromech droid—helper
to Anakin, and later Luke Skywalker:

2DR2

_____

Half alien, half droid, all-around-baddie, and Supreme
Commander of the droid armies:

ARENGLE VIGOREUS

_____

Criminal warlord and father of little "Stinky" Huttlet:

BAJAB HET THUT

_____

Fearless leader of
the clone army:

XER

_____

Jedi Knight and Master
of Anakin Skywalker:

NOWBIA EBINKO

_____

18

PICTURE PERFECT

Count Dooku's secret apprentice Asajj Ventress has several exotic tattoos. Use the space below to design your very own tattoo.

BUILD-A-DROID

R2-D2 and C-3PO have been blasted, bombed, crashed into planets, and torn apart! Study the spare parts below and draw a line to connect them to the correct droid.

MESSAGE TO BASE, MESSAGE TO BASE

Captain Rex's speaker unit has malfunctioned! Decipher this code and pass on the message before it's too late.

_ _ _ _ _ _ _ _

_ _ _ _ _ _ _ _

_ _ _ _ _ _ _ _ _ _ _ _ _ .

A D E H I L N O P R S T U Y

SPOT THE CLONE

The Grand Army of the Republic is being prepared on Kamino. How many clone troopers can you find in the picture below?

_____

AWAY YOUR WEAPON PUT

Each of our heroes and villains has their favorite weapon. Draw in the missing Jedi weaponry and blasters, then color them all in.

STAR WARS® ATTACK!

When you've finished this book, cut out the characters and play this game. Take turns rolling a dice, move the number of spaces shown, and follow the missions you land on. The first player to arrive at MISSION COMPLETE is the winner!

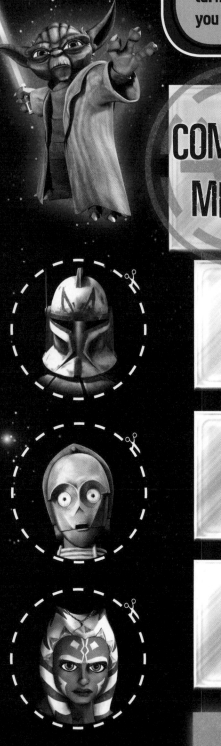

COMMENCE MISSION	2	3	4
18	**17** Jedi Master Count Dooku goes over to the dark side. Move back 1 space.	16	15
19	**20** Jango Fett chosen as clone template. Move another player forward 2 spaces.	21	22
36	35	34	33
37 Battle of Geonosis. Move forward 1 space.	38	39	**40** Separatists unleash the Malevolence. Move back 2 spaces.

5
Blockade of Naboo.
Miss a turn.

6

7

8
Senator Palpatine
elected Chancellor.
Go back to start.

9

14

13
HYPERDRIVE!
Move ahead
6 spaces.

12
Padmé Amidala
seeks help from the
Jedi. Move forward
2 spaces.

11

10

23
HYPERDRIVE!
Move ahead
6 spaces.

24
Obi-Wan Kenobi
warns the Jedi
Council. Move
forward 1 space.

25

26
Mace Windu orders
Anakin to stay
on Tatooine.
Miss a turn.

27

32
Count Dooku recruits
Asajj Ventress.
Move back
1 space.

31

30
Chancellor Palpatine
gains emergency
dictatorial powers. Move
another player back
2 spaces.

29

28

41

42

43
HYPERDRIVE!
Move ahead
1 space.

44

**MISSION
COMPLETE**

MATCHING SQUARES

Cut out the cards on the opposite page and carefully place each one so that it appears once per column and once per row and once per mini-square on each grid. A few of the squares have been filled in to start you off. Good luck and may the Force of logic be with you!

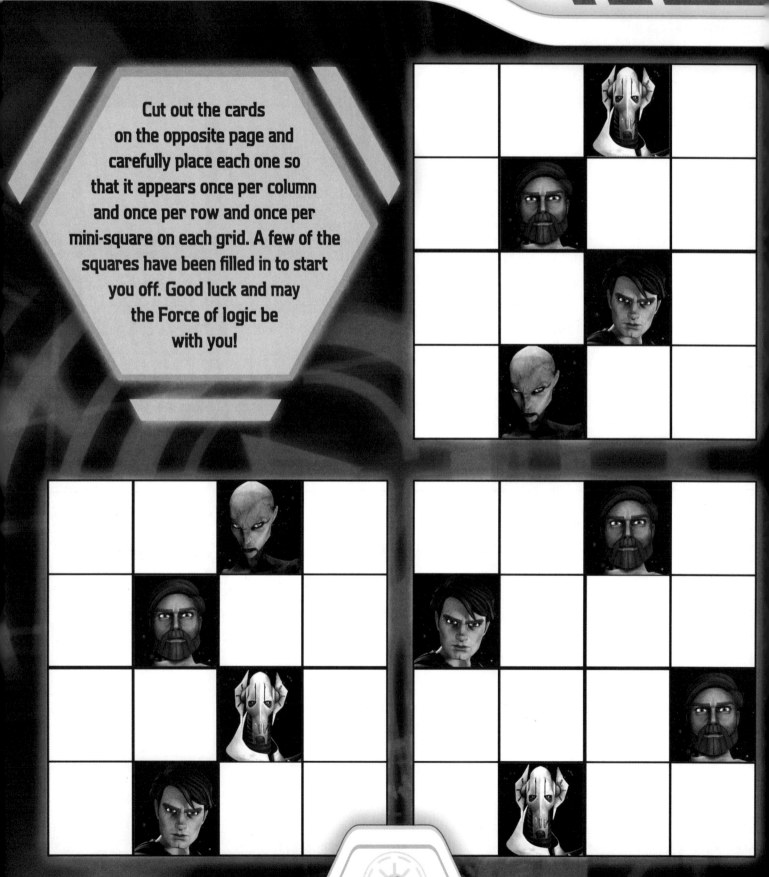

CORELLIAN CROSSWORD

Across

2. Clone captain and friend of Anakin Skywalker (3).
3. Robotic enemies of the clone army (6, 6).
5. Obi-Wan Kenobi and Yoda are part of this group of Knights (4, 7).

Down

1. Mystical power wielded by the Jedi (3, 5).
4. Jedi Council member Mace _____ (5).

JIGSAW JABBA

Jabba the Hutt is trying to get a message through, but there seems to be some interference. Can you work out which of the parts below will complete the picture?

A

B

C

D

E

F

G

H

30

CLONE WARS

Test your Clone Wars knowledge by putting the following armed engagements in the order they were fought. Number them in the boxes to the right of each battle.

ANAKIN DUELS WITH COUNT DOOKU ☐

AHSOKA FIGHTS OFF MAGNAGUARD DROIDS ☐

PADMÉ INFILTRATES ZIRO'S PALACE ☐

OBI-WAN DUELS WITH VENTRESS ☐

ANAKIN AND AHSOKA DUEL WITH VENTRESS ☐

THE BATTLE OF CHRISTOPHSIS ☐

ANSWERS

Page 2
CODE BREAKER
ASAJJ VENTRESS

Page 4
MISSION DEBRIEFING
1. 6
2. Orange
3. Yes
4. 16
5. Blue and Red
6. Green

Page 5
PERILOUS ESCAPE!

Page 6
CRAZY CLONING

Page 7
THE CONSTELLATION
Connect the stars solution: Yoda

Page 12
ON THE DARK SIDE
1. Ahsoka
2. C-3PO
3. Ventress
4. Rex
5. Yoda

Page 13
THE DECODER RING
May the Force be with you.

Page 15
UPSIDE DOWN IN SPACE

Page 18
SIGNAL SCRAMBLE

AHSOKA
R2-D2
GENERAL GRIEVOUS

JABBA THE HUTT
REX
OBI-WAN KENOBI

Page 20
BUILD-A-DROID

Page 21
MESSAGE TO BASE, MESSAGE TO BASE
Palpatine is really Darth Sidious.

Page 22
SPOT THE CLONE
9 clone troopers are hidden in the picture.

Page 26
MATCHING SQUARES

Page 29
CORELLIAN CROSSWORD

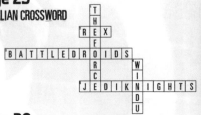

Page 30
JIGSAW JABBA

Page 31
CLONE WARS
The correct battle order is:

1. The Battle of Christophsis
2. Padmé infiltrates Ziro's palace
3. Anakin and Ahsoka duel with Ventress
4. Obi-Wan duels with Ventress
5. Anakin duels with Count Dooku
6. Ahsoka fights off MagnaGuard droids